About the Author

Arabella Florence lives in Northamptonshire, she has enjoyed writing stories and reading books since she was four years old, she fell in love with the local library and it was like her second home.

Arabella says she likes unicorns and rainbows, collecting bugs, dressing up and bouncing on her trampoline, attending birthday parties, especially the cake part. Do you think Arabella has a sweet tooth? She also loves reading books especially the ones with questions at the back!

What does Arabella want to be?

Arabella's favourite toy is a rocket, when she grows up, she wants to zoom off to the moon and collect some rocks to bring back to scientists on Earth and they investigate the rocks and have a cup of tea after a long journey.
What is your favourite toy?

Darcey Duck and The Epic Battle of Buckby

Arabella Florence

Illustrations by Viletta Krutko

Darcey Duck and The Epic Battle of Buckby

Olympia Publishers
London

www.olympiapublishers.com
OLYMPIA PAPERBACK EDITION

A CIP catalogue record for this title is
available from the British Library.

ISBN: 978-1-78830-534-1

First Published in 2020
Olympia Publishers
Tallis House
2 Tallis Street
London
EC4Y 0AB
Printed in Great Britain

Dedication

I wrote this book for my local library, to help raise money to save it from closing down.
I loved playing in the children's groups, dressing up, reading stories and special friends like The Gruffalo and Father Christmas!

Acknowledgements

Thanks to Mummy and Daddy. Thanks to Veta for illustrating my story. Thanks to the publisher for believing in me.
Love Arabella

In a small picturesque village, in the heart of the heartiest
Northamptonshire, stood a statuesque treasured library.
Everybody loved the library, but not as much as Darcey Duck.

Darcey Duck was not an ordinary Duck, she was an extraordinary Duck. No one knew she could read a book, no matter how difficult. She was a brilliant reader!

It happened one day, when the book was left by a pond by a small child, who was fond of books, borrowed from the library.

Darcey Duck was hooked on books.
She carried books in her backpack wherever she went.

On the bus she read.

On the loo she read.

Sitting in the doctor's waiting room she read.

Then she read a sign 'library'. She looked through the window and she couldn't believe what she saw.

"Ooh, Ooh, oh yes! I can't believe how many books there are. This is amazing!" Darcey Duck Jumped for Joy as she imagined millions of books inside the library.

She Joined the library. The library became her second home. The enigmatic of the library coined her. Every day she visited the library, no matter how chaotic her day was. She loved the magic of books!

One day she was out scooting with Derrick Dog. She stopped upon a poster on a log. She got closer and looked up to see a poster. In big bold writing the poster read 'Library to close down!'.

"Ooh big trouble!"
Darcey Duck screamed.
"Ooh, Ooh, oh no! It's
catastrophe."

"Surely they are not going to close the library!" Derrick Dog replied.

"Urgent Assembly!" came a voice.

Everyone one came out of their homes, daddies, mummies, grandparents, brothers, sisters, aunties, uncles and even pets.

"Mayor Trolltherling Ballaloon has announced he is going to shut down our library." Rosie rabbit cried.

"Our library, our home, our treasure." Harriet Horse cried.

"The library is a hub of our community and it would be a real shame to lose such an asset." Roman Rooster said

in his big voice.

"What can we do to save our treasured library?" asked Caitlyn Cat.

"If he wants to shut the library, he is going to have to go through me!" said Pablo Pig.

"Campaign!" suggested Darcey Duck stood in the middle front.

"If we campaign, we should be able to save our library from closure and to do this We need everybody. Can we save our Library? Can we?"

Darcey Duck and the animals chant; "A battle it is. but I am a dragon. My bones rattle not broken. I rise and travel at greater length. I can handle this! Watch me channel my inner strength!

RooooooaaaaaaR!

The children's persistent spirit not broken, they wrote letters to
Mayor Trolltherling Ballaloon, begging him not to close the library.
But letters fell on short sighted Mayor.

Hundreds of animals signed a petition, but Mayor Trolltheling Ballaloon ignored the animals despite their best efforts.

"Ooh, Ooh, oh no!"

"It's catastrophe."

hey were losing trust and faith, ut the important thing is Darcey uck and the animals didn't stop trying.

She thought hard in her sleep.

On the walk.

On the Run in the meadows....

Suddenly, with all that contemplation, she came up with a ginormous idea that was absolutely going to save the treasured library. Darcey Duck read a book, Animal farm by George Orwell and got a brilliant idea.

"Can we save our library? Yes we can!" she concocted a plan.

She talks to Caitlyn Cat. "Meow," Caitlyn Cat agrees.

She talks to Harriet Horse. "Neigh," Harriet Horse Agrees.

She talks to Pablo Pig. "Oink," Pablo Pig Agrees.

She talks to Gracie Goat. "Baaaa," Gracie Goat agrees.

She talks to Derrick Dog. "Woof," Derrick Dog agrees.

She Talks to Roman Rooster. "Cock-a-doodle-doo," Roman Rooster agrees

She talks to Rosie Rabbit. "Sniff," Rosie Rabbit Agrees.

Here comes
Mayor
Trolltherling
Ballaloon!"

The Mayor! On The attack! He's hungry and is after prey. There's panic everywhere. The library is under attack. Should the animals be scared? Should the animals run away and hide?

"Ooh, Ooh, oh no!"

"It's catastrophe!"

"Ooh, Ooh, oh no!" screamed Darcey Duck, her feathers ruffled up.

Suddenly he gets out of the car.
Mayor Trolltheling Ballalloon chuckles an evil
laugh.
A legion of animals await.

"Mayor
Trolltherling
Ballaloon!"

He clears his throat. "I am not interested in what is happening in your village, roads, parking, shops closing down and this?!" The deterioration of the village is your problem not mine. Things are going to get worse.

"what?" Animals in shock.

"This can't be happening."
cried Gracie goat.

"Oh no, I know! Well you have tried and failed."
Mayor Trollthering Ballaloon cackled, hissing
away.

But Darcey Duck so eager on saving the library campaigned even harder. "He is a doubter, the most of them all, who doesn't believe even a tiny winy bit in you that you can do it. He is not a believer; he doesn't believe in you. He thinks it's a waste of time. Then there is you and me proving him wrong, you can do it! Go forth and fight!" Darcey Duck spoke.

"Animals Revolt!"

A legion of animal's rolled out on to an epic battle. Their teeth chattered, their eyes popped out.

BANG, CLANG, BASH, CLASH

Darcey Duck and the Animals marched on, their fighting spirit not broken a tiny winy bit. The quakes, the woofs, the meows, the moos, the neighs, the squeaks and the sniffs through the air.

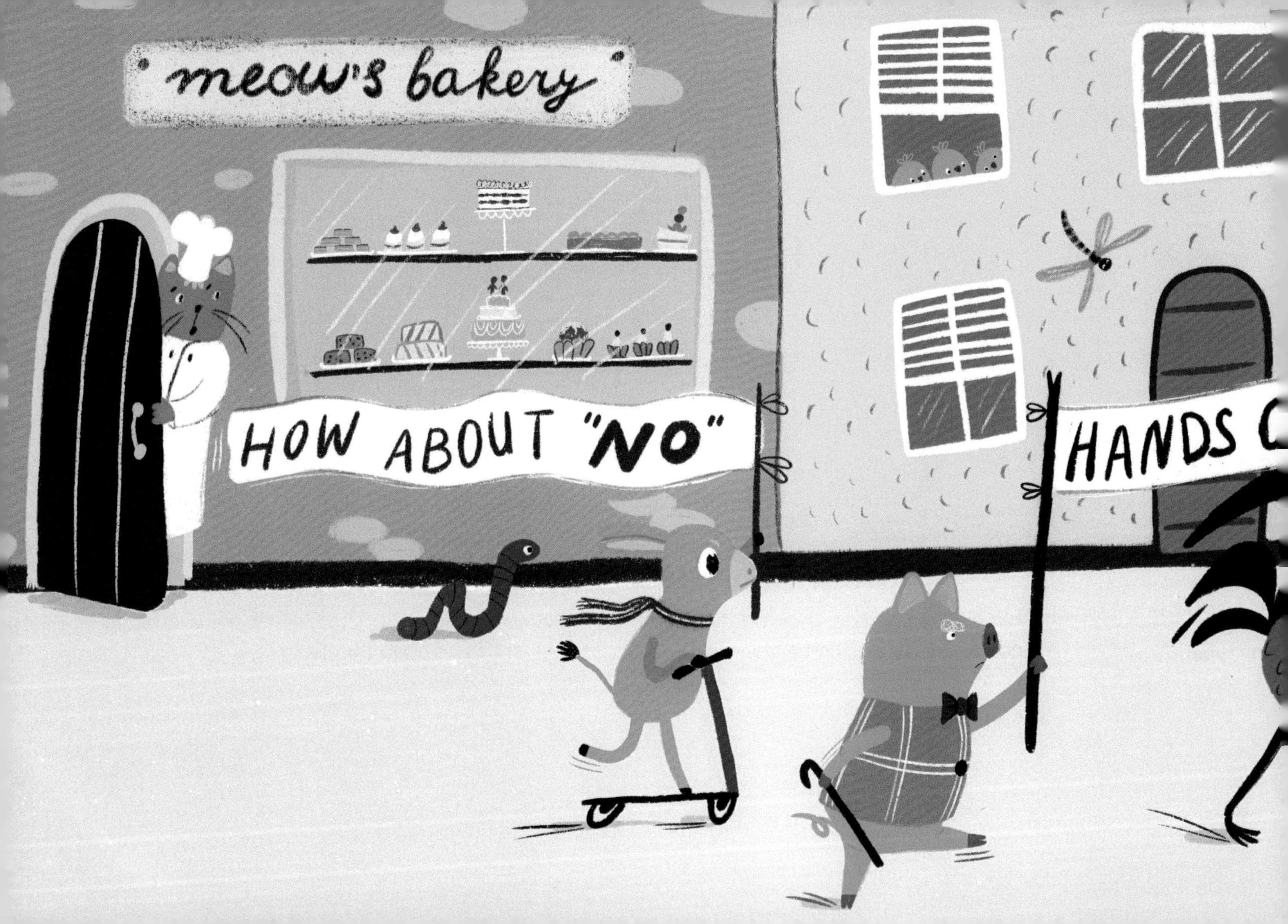
meow's bakery
HOW ABOUT "NO"
HANDS

They marched passed the bakery.

The butchery.

The post office.

Over the bridge they marched

Will Mayor Trolltherling Ballaloon
finally listen? Are they wasting
their time? Should they give up?

The Mayor's office surrounded.
"Ooh, Ooh, oh yes!
We can do it I can do it."
Darcey Duck roared.

Her fighting spirit not broken. Like once the bravest boy with calm who saved his community with no army marching alongside him. With no history before of participation in such action but with his strength and courage combined, he defeated an enormous giant. Then came a declaration.

'If you believe in it and it makes you happy.
Don't stop. Never stop. Keep on fighting!'

The Mayor behind the curtains watched and wobbled with fear. "You don't care about anyone except for yourself," exclaimed Darcey Duck.

"The animals conquered."
He was removed from the office! The helpless and selfless animal's he thought had no power, removed him from office and changed fate of their library and the village thrived again. "Ooh, Ooh, oh yes we can.
We can do it."

Then Darcey Duck and the animals celebrated their victory with a boogie, chanting;
"A battle it is, but I am a dragon. My bones rattle not broken. I rise and travel at greater
#length. I can handle this! Watch me channel my inner strength!"

"Roooooooaaaaaar"

THE END